Duabzong

The Royal Puppy

Written by Judy Katschke
Illustrated by Antonio Campo

Scholastic Inc.

No part of this publication may be reproduced, stored in a retrieval system, or transmitted in any form or by any means, electronic, mechanical, recording, or otherwise, without written permission of the publisher. For information regarding permission, write to Scholastic Inc., Attention: Permissions Department, 557 Broadway, New York, NY 10012.

ISBN 978-0-545-60778-0

HASBRO and its logo, BLYTHE, LITTLEST PET SHOP, and all related characters are trademarks of Hasbro and are used with permission. © 2014 Hasbro. All Rights Reserved. HUB is a trademark of Hub Television Networks, LLC and used with permission.

Published by Scholastic Inc. SCHOLASTIC and associated logos are trademarks and/or registered trademarks of Scholastic Inc.

10 9 8 7 6 5 4 3   14 15 16 17 18 19/0

Designed by Leslie Mechanic
Printed in the U.S.A.   40
First printing, September 2014

Contents

Chapter 1
Royal Welcome Waggin'

"A real-life prince from England visiting Littlest Pet Shop!" Blythe Baxter exclaimed. "I can't believe it!"

It was Saturday morning. Blythe and the pets were waiting for Prince Casper. He would be a day-camper

while the Duke and Duchess toured Downtown City.

"England, huh?" Pepper the skunk said. "Is that why we're wearing go-go boots?"

"It's called the mod look," Blythe explained. "It was trendy in England during the 1960s."

"You mean the *loud* look!" Sunil the mongoose groaned. "My vinyl pants squeak every time I move!"

Blythe smiled. She understood the pets and they understood her, and that was her biggest secret!

It was also no secret Blythe understood fashion. Pet fashion. She even had her own line of clothes at the Littlest Pet Shop called Blythe Style.

Blythe and her dad lived in the same building as Littlest Pet Shop. The store was just a quick ride down the dumbwaiter!

"Blythe, how exciting is this?" Mrs. Twombly called as she rushed over. "We've never had royalty at Littlest Pet Shop before."

The owner of Littlest Pet Shop tapped her chin and added, "Except for that golden retriever named King."

Mrs. Twombly left to speak to reporters. The eager press was camped outside Littlest Pet Shop for the prince!

"What awesome publicity for Littlest Pet Shop!" Blythe said.

"And *me*!" Zoe the spaniel cooed. "Should I strike some glam poses for the pup-arazzi?"

"Speaking of *posers*," Russell the hedgehog whispered. "Here comes trouble times two."

Blythe groaned as Whittany and Brittany Biskit walked over. What did those terrible twins want now?

"Like, you'd better not get used to all this royal hoo-ha, Blythe Baxter," Whittany sniffed.

"What do you mean?" Blythe asked.

"The Duke and Duchess barked up

the wrong tree by picking Littlest Pet Shop!" Whittany said. "It's our dad's store the prince will want."

"Largest Ever Pet Shop?" said Blythe.

Why would Prince Casper choose Fisher Biskit's store instead of Littlest Pet Shop? It was large but definitely not in charge when it came to pets!

"That's Barkingham Palace to you," Whittany said. "Show her, Brittany."

"Like, ta-da!" Brittany said, handing Blythe a tablet.

"What the —?" Blythe gasped. On the screen was Largest Ever Pet Shop redesigned to look like a royal palace!

"Intimidated much?" Whittany said.

"No," Blythe admitted. "Prince Casper will want to have *fun*. And there's nothing fun about all that stuffy-stuff."

Suddenly — WHOOSH!

The twins were swallowed up by a mob of reporters. Blythe and the pets turned to see a sleek gray car pulling up to the curb.

"He's *heeeeeere*!" Minka the monkey cried. "It's Prince Casper!"

Chapter 2
His Royal Highness

The car stopped. Two men wearing blue suits and white gloves hurried out.

"Who are they?" Penny the panda asked.

"They're footmen," Blythe said.

"Yeah, but can they do this fancy footwork?" Vinnie asked as he shuffled his feet.

"Ladies and gentlemen!" one footman shouted. "His Royal canine Highness, Prince Casper!"

A hush fell over the crowd. The footmen opened the car door and revealed a saucer-eyed King Charles  Spaniel. He was wearing a blue velvet suit trimmed with ruffles!

"He's sure dressed for the occasion," Blythe whispered.

"You mean gift-wrapped," Pepper joked.

The footmen carried a doggy throne and trunk as they followed Mrs. Twombly into the store. Blythe and the pets hurried to greet Prince Casper.

"Welcome to Littlest Pet Shop, Prince," Blythe said.

"You can talk to pets?" Casper said, surprised. "In that case, call me 'Your Majesty'."

"How about 'You're Kidding'?" Pepper snapped.

Blythe put her hand over Pepper's mouth. "So, Your Majesty," she said to the prince. "Now that you're here, what

would you like to do for fun?"

"Fun?" Casper said as he blinked with surprise. "I trust you'll think of something to amuse me."

"We will?" Blythe said. Then she quickly added, "Uh — sure we will, Your Majesty!"

"No pressure," Vinnie mumbled.

"In the meantime, I'm ready for high tea," Casper said. "I assume you serve Earl Greyhound."

"I think . . ." Blythe said.

"I'll have mine in a china cup," Casper said.

"He's a barrel of laughs," Vinnie said as Casper entered Littlest Pet Shop. "Maybe he *would* like Barkingham Palace better."

"Don't say that, Vinnie!" Blythe exclaimed. "The prince has to have fun here! Otherwise Littlest Pet Shop will get bad press."

"What if he doesn't know how to have fun?" Penny asked.

"I never thought of that, Penny," Blythe admitted. "No wonder the prince wants us to come up with ideas."

"And who knows more about fun than us?" Zoe said with a smile. "If the prince doesn't know how to have fun, let's show him how!"

"Neat!" Penny exclaimed. "I'll teach him ribbon dancing!"

"I'll tell him jokes!" Pepper said.

"I'll show him how to dance!" Vinnie said as he did a spin . . . and tripped over his tail.

"I'll come up with a

name for our plan," Russell declared. "How about . . . Operation Fun?"

"Like!" Blythe declared. Her friends had saved the day again. "We WILL show Prince Casper how to have fun — the Littlest Pet Shop way!"

Chapter 3
Rocker Spaniel

"Remind me why we're starting with music," Pepper said. "And what's with the little teapot?"

Zoe showed off her latest costume: a pink teapot with a handle and spout.

"Traditions are meant to be shared, Pepper," Zoe explained. "So are my oh-so-fabulous musical numbers and costumes."

"Okay, guys," Blythe whispered. "Let's show Casper what fun really is!"

Casper was sipping his tea as Blythe

and the pets approached the throne.

"Your Majesty!" Zoe announced. "Please welcome the world's favorite doggy diva . . . me!"

Russell cued the music. Casper watched with bored eyes as Zoe began to sing.

When life throws you lemons,
here's what to do.
Make life a tea party.
One lump or two?

Casper's ears suddenly perked up. "What is that sound?" he asked. "It seems to be coming from outside."

Blythe and the pets followed Casper to the front window.

"What?" Blythe cried.

On the sidewalk there was a string quartet.

The Biskits were dancing to the music while wearing gowns and towering white wigs!

"Like, why are we dancing the mosquito net, Whittany?" Brittany complained.

"Brittany, it's the *minuet* — a fancy, old dance," Whittany snapped. "And stop stepping on my feet!"

"So that's their plan," Russell said. "If Casper won't visit Barkingham Palace — the palace will visit Casper!"

Prince Casper sighed as he watched the Biskits. "I've seen this dance before," he said slowly, "back home at the palace."

"Uh-oh," Penny whispered. "What if the Biskits are making Casper homesick with their dancing?"

"Or just plain sick?" Pepper joked.

Blythe frowned. Whatever the Biskits' plan was, it wouldn't work. Not if she and the pets could help it!

"Casper WILL have fun at the Littlest Pet Shop," Blythe insisted. She then gave a shrug. "As soon as we figure out HOW!"

Chapter 4
Slick Trick

"I thought they'd never go!" Blythe said after the Biskits and musicians packed up and left.

"Blythe?" Mrs. Twombly asked, walking over. "Is Prince Casper enjoying himself? He seems so serious!"

Blythe gulped. She didn't want Mrs. T. to know about Barkingham

Palace or Operation Fun.

"Um — that's because he's *seriously* enjoying himself," Blythe blurted.

Mrs. Twombly shrugged as she began walking away. "Okeydokey," she said. "Let the good times roll."

Blythe and the pets waited until Mrs. T. was out of earshot.

"Even Mrs. Twombly knows Casper isn't happy," Blythe groaned. "What are we going to do?"

"It's going to take magic to turn Casper's frown upside down," Penny said.

Magic? Blythe smiled. *That's it!*

"Sunil?" Blythe asked. "Will you put on a magic show for the prince?"

"A royal performance?" Sunil cried. "What if the prince doesn't like my magic? He could make me disappear!"

"Or he can make you a royal magician," Pepper said slowly. "If he likes your magic, that is."

Sunil's eyes lit up. "What's not to like?" he cried. "Get me my cape!"

Soon Sunil stood before Prince Casper. He stuck his hand inside his tall hat.

"Next he'll pull out a rabbit," Casper sighed. "How painfully predictable."

"Behold, Your Majesty!" Sunil shouted. His eyes widened as he yanked out not a rabbit but a box of DVDs!

"Masterpup Theatre?" Sunil said, reading the box. "How did those DVDs get in here?"

"I watch Masterpup Theatre back at the palace," Casper said. "It's quite . . . posh."

A card dropped out from between the DVDs. Pepper read it aloud: "Compliments of Barkingham Palace."

"Barkingham Palace?" Casper said curiously."

Pepper quickly shoved the note inside Sunil's mouth before Casper could see it.

"Abraca-doodle!" she said. "The great Sunil made it disappear!"

Blythe stared at Casper sulking on his throne.

The prince was still not a happy camper. And if he visited Barkingham Palace the press would have a field day!

"We have to get back to the drawing board!" Blythe insisted.

Russell's quills perked up.

"Did you say drawing board?" Russell said. He stroked his prickly chin thoughtfully. "I think I have an idea."

Chapter 5
Minka's Mess-terpiece

"Are you sure this will work, Russell?" Blythe asked. She looked at Casper, who was now dressed in an artist's smock.

"There's nothing like art to loosen up a pet," Russell assured. "And what better pet for the job than our own artist, Minka?"

"That's *meeee*!" Minka cried.

"If we're going to paint," Casper said, "where is my paintbrush?"

"Who needs a paintbrush?" Minka

exclaimed. "Dig in and hurl!"

Casper yelped as Minka began flinging gobs of paint at the canvas!

"You're making a mess!" Casper shouted. "Stop it at once!"

Minka stopped just as Mrs. Twombly walked over.

"Special delivery for His Highness!"

Mrs. Twombly said. She leaned a flat package wrapped in brown paper against the wall.

As Mrs. T. walked back to the counter, Blythe stared at the package. Was it another Biskit bombshell?

"Don't open it!" Blythe said.

Too late. The paper dropped off. Underneath was a gold-framed portrait of Whittany and Brittany. Sitting at their feet was Casper!

"It's a royal portrait like the ones back home," Casper said as he studied the painting. "And it's signed by Barkingham Palace."

"So?" Pepper asked.

"So maybe I should visit this Barkingham Palace . . . " Casper muttered. "It's not like I'm having any fun here."

Blythe and the pets gasped. Was this the end of the royal visit to Littlest Pet Shop?

Chapter 6
Clothes Call

"Time is running out, you guys," Blythe said. "Any more ideas? *Pleeeeeease?*"

"Pepper is telling Casper jokes!" Russell said. "That might do the trick."

The bells on Pepper's jester cap jingled as she said, "Your Majesty, what do dragons play soccer with?"

"What?" Casper sighed.

"Fireballs!" Pepper said.

Everyone laughed except Casper.

"I've never seen dragons play soccer," Casper said.

"What's with this guy?" Pepper groaned.

Vinnie tried next . . .

"If you ask me, Prince," Vinnie said. "You should be dancing!"

Vinnie pulled Casper off his throne. But the princely pup stood absolutely statue-stiff!

"Casper is just too stuffy to get scruffy," Zoe sighed.

Stuffy? Blythe stared at Casper's ruffles and stiff collar.

"That's what's keeping Casper from having fun!" Blythe exclaimed. "His clothes!"

Chapter 7
Pets to the Dress-cue!

"And here's Russell," Blythe announced. "Modeling what all the well-dressed princes will be wearing this year!" Russell pivoted in khaki pants and a polo shirt. Blythe had designed comfy but chic outfits for Casper lickety-split. The pets had helped by sewing and now modeling!

"Your fashion show is a waste of time," Casper said. "Princes must wear royal clothes"

Pepper pointed to Casper's sleeve. "Looks like Minka got a little paint on your royal cuff," she said.

"Princes must wear clean clothes, too!" Casper gasped. He grabbed one of Blythe's outfits and changed behind the throne. Seconds later he stepped out looking sharp, casual, and stunned.

"What do you think?" Blythe asked.

"What do I think?" Casper asked.

Blythe held her breath. Until Casper broke into a whirl of cartwheels!

"I think I want to chase squirrels!"

Casper exclaimed. "And catch tennis balls in the park! And roll in leaves until I smell like a *dog*!"

"Score!" the pets cheered.

"So . . . you don't want to visit Barkingham Palace, Your Majesty?" Blythe asked.

"Absolutely not!" Casper declared.

"But you said it's just like home," Penny said.

"It IS just like home — BOR-RING!"

Casper exclaimed. He turned another cartwheel. "But with comfy clothes like these — I can finally have fun!"

"Then what are we waiting for?" Blythe declared. "Let's hit the town and play!"

When Blythe and the pets returned to Littlest Pet Shop, Mrs. Twombly was scratching her head.

"I don't get it," Mrs. Twombly said. "People are calling and asking for clothes just like Prince Casper's!"

Casper stepped out from behind Blythe. When Mrs. T. saw him covered with leaves and dirt, she gasped: "Cheese and crackers! What have you done to the prince?"

Chapter 8
London Calling

"Seriously, Mrs. T.," Blythe started to say. "Casper's clothes were —"

"Phooey-kablooey!" Mrs. Twombly cried, glancing out the window. "The Duke and Duchess are here for Casper!"

The royal car was parked outside, and the Duke and Duchess were at the door!

"I know we're a day early, Mrs. Twombly," the Duchess said as they walked inside. "But we received the most mysterious text."

"It was from two people, a Whittany and a Brittany," the Duke said, "advising us to pick up our dog immediately!"

The Duke gasped at Casper and said, "Is *that* our dog? He's not dressed like our dog."

"W-w-well," said Mrs. Twombly with a stammer in her voice.

"He doesn't *act* like our dog, either," the Duchess said, pointing to Casper doing cartwheels. "He seems *happy*!"

"And that makes *us* happy!" The Duke smiled.

"So, you like Casper's new look?" Blythe asked.

"We do indeed!" the Duke declared.

"The Queen likes dressing pets in royal attire," the Duchess said. "But the Duke and I prefer the casual look."

"I believe Casper does, too!" the Duke added.

That gave Blythe an idea . . .

"How about I design an official line of Prince Casper pet fashions?" Blythe said. "You know, you don't have to be a royal pup to look like one!"

"Brilliant!" the Duke and Duchess cried.

"We can sell the clothes in Littlest Pet Shop," Mrs. Twombly said excitedly. "And all over the world!"

Mrs. Twombly ran to call the press. The royal couple turned to Blythe.

"You've done so much for Casper," the Duke said. "We'd like to invite you and the pets to our palace in England."

"What do you think?" the Duchess asked.

"Brilliant!" Blythe gasped. I mean, thank you, Your Majesties!"

"Should we send the royal plane?" the Duchess asked.

"No, thank you," Blythe said with a smile. "I have something just as cool. A pilot dad!"

Blythe and the pets walked the royals to their car. Everybody was in a good mood, except for Whittany and Brittany Biskit! They were on the sidewalk holding a giant British flag, hoping to get Prince Caspar's attention. But it didn't take long for them to realize that their dream of rubbing paws with royalty was crushed. As the car sped off, a gust of wind tangled up the twins in the flag. Now their flag was crushed, too.

"We're going to England!" Blythe cheered as she and the pets walked back into the store. "How amazingly cool is that?"

"Way cool!" Russell agreed.

It didn't take long for Blythe to imagine all the adventures that she

would have with the day campers in England.

"Let's celebrate!" Zoe suggested. "How about Earl Greyhound tea, all around?"

"Tea?" Blythe asked.

Zoe hopped onto Casper's throne. She leaned all the way back and smiled.

"Some traditions were meant to be shared," Zoe said. "And this is one I can definitely get used to!"